The latin name for the lion is *Panthera leo*

I ♥ Lions

All lion cubs are born with blue eyes, which change to brown when they are about 3 months old.

Female lions are usually the hunters in the pride. The males protect the territory where they live.

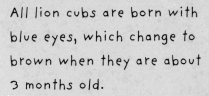

The growing human population means that much of the lions' habitat is being converted into settlements and agriculture. This means there is less prey for the lions to hunt.

The roar of an adult male can be heard up to 5 miles away.

A big male lion can weigh up to 440lbs. Females are usually lighter, weighing around 286lbs.

For Sienna and Monet
Be more Lion! xx

First published in 2021 by Child's Play (International) Ltd
Ashworth Road, Bridgemead, Swindon SN5 7YD, UK

First published in USA in 2021 by Child's Play Inc
250 Minot Avenue, Auburn, Maine 04210

Distributed in Australia by Child's Play Australia Pty Ltd
Unit 10/20 Narabang Way, Belrose, Sydney, NSW 2085

ISBN 978-1-78628-633-8
SJ110621CPL08216338

Printed in Shenzhen, China

1 3 5 7 9 10 8 6 4 2

A catalogue record of this book
is available from the British Library

www.childs-play.com

Bea by the Sea

Jo Byatt

Bea loved lions.
No one knew more about lions than Bea!

Bea thought about lions all day long.

What do they eat for breakfast?

Would lions like a bubbly bath?

Do lions visit the dentist?

How many teeth do they have?

How fast can lions run?

One day Mom said,
"It's a lovely morning.
Let's go to the beach!"

"Do we have to?" asked Bea. "Can't we just stay and play here?"

Bea didn't like sand at all.
It was too gritty, too sticky,
and too scratchy, especially
when it got between her toes.

Bea put her boots on,
and packed her lion stuff.

"I'll pretend I'm a lion,"
she thought.
"They aren't afraid
of anything!"

Bea was a bit wobbly, but she managed to hop from rock to rock without touching any sand.

"Wow!" exclaimed Mom. "Look at those sand sculptures! They're amazing!"

But Bea was far too busy not touching the sand.

All of a sudden, she tripped over something and fell flat on her face.

In the sand!

Bea frantically
brushed the sand
off her face.

"Hello!
I'm Sand Lion,"
boomed
a loud voice.
"Who are you?"

"I'm Bea," she replied.
"I don't like sand,
and I'm covered in it!
And where's my boot?"

"You're missing out,"
replied Sand Lion.
"Come and see!"

"Making footprints in the sand is much better with your boots off!" explained Sand Lion.

"Ooh!" Bea squealed.
"It feels so scratchy!"

Sand Lion thought she was doing really well.

They listened to the sound of the sea.

"It's just like your roar!" giggled Bea.

They built a giant sandcastle.

They made a big sand angel. And a little sand angel.

Until Bea was covered in sand!

"I guess sand isn't so bad," said Bea.
"But I think I'll wash it off my hands now."
She looked up. "What's the matter, Sand Lion?"

"I really don't like water," he shivered.

"It's okay when you get used to it," said Bea.
"Let's try jumping over these little waves."

Bea thought Sand Lion was doing really well.

At the end of the day, it was time to go home.

"The tide's coming in!"
Mom shouted. "Let's go, Bea!"

"See you tomorrow,
Sand Lion!" smiled Bea.
"We'll have such fun!"

The next morning, Bea couldn't wait to get to the beach.

"Slow down!" laughed Mom.
"I thought you didn't like sand?"

But when they arrived there was
nothing left of the sand sculptures.
The sandcastle had gone.

And Sand Lion
had disappeared, too!

Bea felt sad. She sat down on the sand
and looked out to sea. The roar of the waves
reminded her of Sand Lion's voice.

She remembered all the fun they'd had...

...and she knew just what to do.

Sand is created by the weathering and erosion of rocks over thousands of years. As global warming causes sea levels to rise, many beaches will disappear.

The tallest sandcastle ever built (so far!) measured 58ft. It was built in Germany in 2019.

Sand can be:

white ✓
red ✓
black ✓
brown ✓
yellow ✓
pink ✓

Sea turtles return to the same beach each year to lay their eggs in the sand. The gender of a baby sea turtle is determined by the temperature of the sand the eggs are laid in.

The longest beach is in Brazil. It is about 150 miles long.